Praise for Storyshares

"One of the brightest innovators and game-changers in the education industry."
— Forbes

"Your success in applying research-validated practices to promote literacy
serves as a valuable model for other organizations seeking to create
evidence-based literacy programs."   — Library of Congress

"We need powerful social and educational innovation, and Storyshares is
breaking new ground. The organization addresses critical problems facing
our students and teachers. I am excited about the strategies it brings to the
collective work of making sure every student has an equal chance in life."
— Teach For America

"It's the perfect idea. There's really nothing like this. I mean, wow, this will be a
wonderful experience for young people."   — Andrea Davis Pinkney,
Executive Director, Scholastic

"Reading for meaning opens opportunities for a lifetime of learning. Providing
emerging readers with engaging texts that are designed to offer both challeng-
es and support for each individual will improve their lives for years to come.
Storyshares is a wonderful start."
— David Rose, Co-founder of CAST & UDL

Sparkle in the Sea

Storyshares presents

Published by Storyshares, LLC

Storyshares
Storyshares, LLC
24 N. Bryn Mawr Avenue #340
Bryn Mawr, Pennsylvania 19010-3304
www.storyshares.org

Inspiring reading with a new kind of book.

Interest Level: High School
Grade Level Equivalent: 3.8

ISBN 9798885977906
Book design by Saskia Globig

SPARKLE
in the SEA

Natasa Glisic First

Storyshares

CONTENTS

CHAPTER 1

"No, it's not good. Again," Ana muttered to herself.

She could freely shout out loud because there was no one around, but that wouldn't help her either. She put down the palette and stared at the sea in front of her.

Why didn't she just admit the obvious fact? She would never become a "real" painter, one with an arts degree. She just wasn't talented enough. No one was impressed by her sunset landscape painting at the entrance exam for the Paris Academy of Fine Arts.

"Technically it's not bad, but something is missing. It seems like you were painting with feelings separated from the painting. You can't feel the soul. Yes, that's right. There is no soul," a member of the examination committee had said.

That comment hurt her, because she was painting that setting sun with all her soul.

For Ana, going to the Paris Academy would be the first step to professional painting and an independent life in a new city, separated from her mother. Finally, no one would bother her for spending too much time painting. She would no longer have to explain herself to anyone. She could live her life and be completely free!

That's why she threw herself into creating a new painting when the Paris Academy of Fine Arts announced that the winner of the September competition in landscape painting would be admitted to the Academy.

If she could win, all her dreams would come true. And she would win, she was sure, if only she managed to paint the right color of the sea.

She sighed loudly.

CHAPTER 2

Ana decided to paint the place that meant the most to her in the world: the Bay of Waves. It was the name of a very small bay, hidden by rocks and tall pine trees. It was the perfect place to sunbathe and the perfect place to swim.

She was completely enchanted by the color of the sea. It was not bright blue like the sea in the Maldives, or green like the sea in the Mediterranean. This was a special mix of those two colors.

She assumed that the color was because of the bottom of the sea, which was a mixture of pebbles and flat rocks. When it was sunny and clear, the sunlight reflected off of the bottom of the sea and made a unique shade of blue-green. She mixed paints of every blue and green shade that could be found on her planet and never once came close to matching the sea of the Bay of Waves.

Like everyone who painted, Ana knew the place where pigments in every possible color could be bought. From what she saw in the store's catalog, they weren't too expensive either. The problem was that the place was on the distant planet of Ketan.

The teleporter took about fifteen minutes to get from Earth to Ketan. The price of that trip was too expensive for her. Her budget covered only the cost of a round-trip ticket for the cheapest kind of transport: the rocket.

She put her things in her backpack and re-turned home. Fortunately, her mom hadn't returned yet, so she checked the balance of her bank account in peace.

She had installed her own account on the home robot with her own password, without her mom's knowledge. That turned out to be useful. Mom didn't see the warning Ana had received from the city for throwing paper in the street.

She had to enroll into the Academy. And she had to do everything to make it work.

CHAPTER 3

Ana stood in line and patiently waited for her turn to board the rocket. Ten more people to go.

It was warm, and all the passengers were dressed in light summer clothes. Everyone had a monitor under the skin of their wrist. All they had to do was hold their wrists up to the ticket reader, but for some reason the reader was slow.

Maybe all of this was ordinary for those who traveled by rocket?

This was Ana's first interplanetary trip, and she had no experience. Would the reader load her ticket? What if it broke down just as it was her turn? What if she couldn't travel because of that? What if...?

She shook her head. She had to push those thoughts out of her mind. She should concentrate on something positive. Relaxing.

She looked at the gray building next to her airstrip. A teleporter. No people could be seen at the entrance. Everything seemed quiet and efficient.

Black limousines would silently glide to the entrance and lower to the ground. Then the rear door would open and a person, sometimes more than one, would get out of the vehicle and walk into the building. The limousines would float away after that and everything was calm again.

Two more people to go. Ana carefully watched what they were doing. When it was her turn, she did exactly the same. After a few seconds, the text appeared on the reader:

Ana Marija Sassi Rizich
Planet Earth, Europe, 18 years old
Seat: 32 A RIGHT
Destination: Koo' choorb, planet Ketan

She had panicked for no reason. It was kid stuff. You put your monitor on the reader and waited for your name and seat number to appear on the reader. The reader was simply slow. It probably had an outdated software version and had a hard time reading wrist monitors.

CHAPTER 4

She entered the rocket and looked for her seat.
The inside of the rocket looked like the airplanes
people used to travel across the Earth. As far as
she could see, the difference was in the shape
and size of the seats. Here, they looked like deck
chairs with mattresses and had three pairs of wide
belts each. Security reasons. No one wanted other
passengers floating uncontrollably over their head
during weightlessness.

The rocket was half empty. Maybe the planet
Ketan, its destination, did not create much interest
in visiting?

Actually, the planet Ketan was very popular.
It was the most developed planet in their galaxy.

Whatever someone needed—technology, culture, minerals—they would find it on Ketan. Ketan had a reputation for having the best of the best.

"For you? How about the latest learning app?" the robot flight attendant asked Ana. He sounded like her mom when she was trying to talk Ana into something.

"No, thanks," she answered. "I would like to sleep."

"Of course," the robot attendant said. "We can offer you sleeping during the whole trip, sleeping during half the trip, and occasional sleeping."

"Sleeping during the entire trip, please," she said.

The hatch on the robot's body opened. A glass filled with some liquid appeared.

"Here you are, Ana Marija Sassi Rizich. The sleeping water is adapted to your age, weight, height, blood type, and DNA," the robot attendant said.

She took the glass and drank it all at once. She imagined that this was how an experienced interplanetary traveler behaved. She put the cup back into the robot's body and adjusted the seat to a reclining position.

CHAPTER 5

"Can I offer you a lullaby, a bedtime story, a plush friend?" the robot asked. It wouldn't leave her alone.

"No, thanks. This is perfect for me," Ana interrupted him. She turned her back on him, a clear sign that she wanted to be left alone.

The robot attendant made a coughing sound.

"Yes?" she asked, irritated. What was not clear to him?

"I noticed that you are not wearing an oxygen mask. Can I offer you two versions of the oxygen mask?" the robot attendant asked.

Oh, what a fool! She had completely forgotten about the mask!

SPARKLE IN THE SEA

There was no oxygen in the rocket during the flight, and Ketan had its own atmosphere. Earthlings had to use masks to breathe.

"Yes, thank you," she said. Ana tried to sound casual, even though her face was burning with heat. She must have been as red as paprika.

"I can offer you a mask with a duration of five days," the robot said.

"No, I need something shorter," she said.

She counted quickly to herself. A one-way rocket trip would take one day. With the return, it was two days. She just had to go to the first store with painting accessories and buy blue-green pigment. She didn't plan to spend the night on Ketan. She didn't have money for such a luxury. So, a total of two-and-and-a-half days.

"A mask for two-and-and-a-half days, please," she said.

"I can offer you a mask with a duration of five days," repeated the robot.

"No, I don't need that," Ana said. "A mask for two-and-and-a-half days, please."

"I can offer you a five-day mask," the robot repeated, like a parrot.

"Do you offer masks that last less than five days?" she asked.

"Currently, I only offer masks with a duration of five days," the robot attendant said.

She bit her tongue to keep herself from yelling at the robot. It wasn't its fault; it was simply programmed that way.

"A mask with a duration of five days, please," she said.

She placed her wrist on the robot's forehead and confirmed the purchase of the oxygen mask. The robot's body opened again, this time with a mask.

"Can I offer you a mask fitting service?" the robot attendant asked.

"No, thanks," Ana said. "I'll do it myself. I want to sleep now." The robot did not move away from her until she adjusted the mask on her face and turned it on. Only then did it leave.

She rubbed the monitor on her wrist and logged into her bank account. The mask had cost her more than she'd planned. The next cost would have to be the pigment. Then, if there was something left for food, great. If not, it didn't matter. She could go a day without food.

CHAPTER 6

Soft music woke Ana up. The rocket cabin was filled with light.

"Welcome to Ketan, dear passengers. The trip went perfectly. When leaving the rocket, we ask passengers to sort themselves according to their final destination. Air-trains are located to the left of the rocket exit," the announcement said.

Ana felt perfect, rested and full of energy. She stretched and sat down.

The passengers around her acted the same way. Everyone was smiling at each other.

"It's the mask," the nearest passenger said to her with a smile. "The air we breathe is adapted to the character of the Ketans. Wise creatures, Ketans. There is no hostility or aggression on Ketan. Everyone who wears masks breathes an air of peace."

Her mom would call it an illegal drug. She laughed at the thought and exited the rocket in good spirits.

Koo' choorb was written on her wrist. The man next to her had the same sign, so she decided to follow him and do everything he did. He had obviously been to Ketan many times because he moved skillfully through the crowd.

Ana was ready to meet other types of beings, but this landing pad was only for planet Earth. Only Earthlings seemed to use rockets to travel.

The man entered the train and Ana jumped after him. This train was unusual. Instead of chairs, it had tall pods without lids. The man in front of her opened one, entered, and closed the door. Only his masked head was sticking out above the pod.

She opened the pod next to his and entered, but her head was not sticking out. The pod was too tall. She got out of the pod and looked around. All the passengers' heads were popping out.

What now? She would have to ask someone for help, and she didn't like that at all. Everyone would think she was ignorant.

CHAPTER 7

She looked around the train in panic. The pods were filling up quickly. There were no handrails on this train, only pods.

"There, the one over there is free. See?" a woman next to her said, and pointed her finger. The woman's pod was shorter than the others. Obviously, there were pods of different heights. A green light flashed above the pod she pointed to, a sign that it was free.

"Thank you!" Ana said quickly. She hurried to the pod.

She nervously entered the pod and realized that it was up to her chin. Excellent! Now her head was sticking out above the pod, like the others.

"Attention! Attention! We're leaving in five seconds," the announcement said, in Earthlings' language.

Ana's pod started to shrink! Would it crush her?

The same was happening to others, but no one seemed terrified. In fact, someone even hummed a song out loud. The case narrowed right up to Ana's body and stopped. She guessed it was supposed to be like that.

Five seconds passed. Ana prepared herself to move, but nothing happened. The train was standing still.

"Time on Ketan lasts longer than on Earth. Seconds last like minutes," a new friendly traveler near her explained.

She wondered, *Why aren't people so kind on Earth?*

"Thank you," she said politely.

As they started, her body suddenly leaned forward, probably from the speed. She stuck to the inside of the pod and was in that position for a few minutes. Then she leaned back, a sign of the train slowing down. Her body went back to a normal, upright position. The pod moved away from her body.

She had arrived at *Koo' choorb.*

CHAPTER 8

"Ah, this is only possible on Ketan! In our country, even airplanes do not travel at this speed. Wonderful people, Ketans," someone said next to her.

Ana got out of the train and her eyes widened in wonder. She only saw humans in her life on Earth. She had never seen Ketans or Notors, beings from the planet Notor. For her, they had always been in photos and videos. Now, she was surrounded by them.

The Ketans were dressed in very little clothing. Their light-gray skin shone in the bright sunlight. They moved gracefully, with elegant body movements. They were similar to humans, of course, since they were direct descendants of humans. But the Ketans were thought to be a perfected version of humans. They were much more intelligent and peaceful than humans.

The painting supply store was located near the train station. Ana looked at the instructions on her wrist. She had entered the address of the store while she was on Earth and then turned on the navigator. It all seemed so long ago and far away. She was finally on Ketan! She was filled with such happiness and joy that she wanted to scream, but that was not possible with the mask on her face. Besides, she would probably upset everyone around her. There was laughter and chatter, but nothing loud.

She went out of the building and into the street. Everything was very similar to Earth, and yet completely different. The sky was pale gray and the sun was shining more intensely. The Ketans moved easily through the streets without shelter, while canopies were provided for the Earthlings.

The streets were covered with gray grass, and the unusual trees without leaves were gray too. They sparkled like they were covered in glitter. She also saw plants from Earth in some places. They were covered by large transparent domes, protected from the sun and in the necessary atmosphere.

The buildings were also gray, but the shops' windows were full of incredibly colorful items they sold.

She followed the navigator's instructions. Soon her wrist was flickering. It read:

You have arrived at your destination. Your destination is right in front of you.

And indeed it was. In the shop window was a wide variety of paint brushes, field and table easels, canvases, palettes, and everything else that an artist could wish for.

This was it. The place where her destiny was about to be fulfilled.

Her heart started to pound harder. She entered the store.

CHAPTER 9

"Good afternoon." A salesgirl immediately greeted her at the entrance.

"Good afternoon," she answered politely.

The space was much bigger than she expected. Everything was sorted and neatly stacked so that the customer could find their way around easily. The only problem was that everything was written in the Ketan language, which Ana did not understand. She put her wrist to the description of one brush, but all she got was:

Error. Try again.

Her processor did not have an out-of-Earth language option. Of course, she could upgrade it.

She would just have to pay for it, with money she didn't have.

She looked around to find someone who could help her. Everyone here was smiling at her like they couldn't wait to help.

"Excuse me," she said to an older Ketan.

"Hello, how may I help you?" he quickly answered in her language.

"I am looking for a pigment of a special color, blue-green," Ana said. "Do you know where it is?"

"Blue-green? A beautiful color, indeed," the Ketan said. "I chose yellow and orange, like your sun on Earth. Colors of the icy sun."

She didn't understand. Icy sun? To who was the sun icy?

"You don't work here?" she asked him.

"No," he laughed. "I'm sorry. Yellow and orange are in this row. And the salesman is over there. In gray clothes."

"Thank you very much," Ana said.

Gray clothes? Everyone was in gray!

"Excuse me," she asked a man whom she hoped was a salesman.

"How can I help you?" he asked.

"Do you work here? Are you a salesperson?" she asked, to check.

"Yes, how can I help you?" the man asked again.

"I'm looking for a blue-green pigment," Ana said.

"Can you be more specific?" he asked. "Got a code? Name?"

"Yes, the name is N'gao gaao," she said.

"N'gao gaao?" he repeated and looked up. He was probably searching the store stock using a chip embedded in his head. "Yes, we do have it. What quantity do you need?"

"Two packs," she said.

The salesman left and returned in one minute.

"Here are the pigments. You know how to deal with them, right? They have a special opener. I will open it now with the key and you have exactly one day to use them," he said.

"What do you mean by one day?" Ana asked.

"This pigment is very unstable," the man said. "It changes color if it is exposed to the Earth's atmosphere for more than a day."

"But I need one day just to return to Earth. I can't make it in one day!" she said, beginning to panic.

"I'm very sorry," he said. "This pigment can only be opened with a special key. Ketans who have a color certificate are the only ones allowed to have pigment keys. Only they can open this pigment for you. Are there any certified Ketans on Earth at this time?"

"I do not know," she barely answered. "Can I borrow the key, so I can open the pigment myself?"

"Certainly not. Only certified Ketans have the key, and only they use it," he said.

"But... But... I need that pigment. Do you have a pigment package that can last a day and a half?" Ana asked.

"Of course, but not these blue-green shades. Do you want me to show you?" he asked.

"No. Thank you," she stammered. Her eyes filled with tears.

Was it possible that everything was over before it actually started? That all her effort was for nothing? She hoped so much, wanted so much... Everything turned out to be pointless.

Nothing would ever become of her. Mom used to tell her that she was foolish and irresponsible. She was right.

CHAPTER 10

"Dad, what is this?" the salesgirl asked. She pointed her finger at Ana's face.

"Tears. When humans are very sad, they look like this," he explained to her.

"Oh..." the girl said.

"You stay with her, and I'll go help other customers," he said to the salesgirl, his daughter.

Turning to Ana, he said, "Let me know what you decide about the pigment."

The salesgirl watched Ana without saying a word. She was about Ana's age, with intense yellow eyes and dark-red hair.

"I'm Vri," said the salesgirl.

Ana didn't react.

She left the store. She would go back to the rocket. She had failed. Her dream of becoming a professional painter was dead.

"Hey, wait!" a voice said behind her.

It was the young salesgirl, Vri.

"Where are you going?" Vri asked her.

"Back to Earth," Ana said.

"How about we go to Earth's park while you are still here?" Vri suggested.

Ana shrugged. She didn't care. She no longer had a future.

Vri bought a ticket to enter the park, a huge, transparent dome. Inside was a typical park from Earth: trees, wooden benches, green grass, flowers.

"This is my favorite place in the city. Let's sit on a bench. It's so nice," Vri said. She looked around, admiring the park.

Ana just shrugged her shoulders without saying a word. It was nothing special to her.

"Why do you need that one pigment? Take some similar one," Vri suggested.

"I can't. I want to paint my sea. My sea is that color. Unique," Ana sighed.

"Why do you want to paint that particular sea? Why not something else?" asked Vri.

36

"Because that bay is very important to me," Ana answered. "That's where I learned to swim. That's where I first went night swimming. That's where I... Well, there was a guy I liked, and so... You know. I don't have to draw it for you."

"Draw?" Vri asked.

"Well, that's just how we humans say it when we don't want to talk about details," Ana said.

Silence.

Ana had insulted kind and friendly Vri. Vri didn't deserve it.

"Okay. Okay," she explained. "It was moonlight, and that guy and I were sitting on the beach and talking. Then he hugged me. We talked a little more, and then we started kissing. Just like that, out of nothing! It was wonderful. We kissed and cuddled."

"And then?" Vri's yellow eyes were wide open.

"And then? Nothing. We went home. The next day, I saw him on another beach with another girl," Ana said.

She shrugged. Apparently, kissing in the moonlight was only wonderful for her.

CHAPTER 11

"And what about you?" Ana asked.

"Me?" Vri asked, looking surprised.

"Yes, you. Do you like someone?" Ana asked.

"No, it's different here. We don't have kisses," Vri said. "We don't touch each other at all. The feeling of my skin next to someone else's is not a pleasant feeling. Somehow... it scratches; it gets stuck. I can't explain it. We don't kiss, nothing like that. Here, when you love someone, you go to the clinic and make a child."

"What clinic?" Ana asked.

"Well, for having children. A skin sample is taken from a couple, and a child is made according to the wishes of the parents," said Vri. "Take me, for example. It was difficult to find the gene for yellow eyes in my family, but my parents really wanted it, so they paid for extra tests. Yellow eyes are not common on Ketan. Here, they are mostly green and blue. No one has black eyes like yours. They are very beautiful to me."

Now it was clearer to Ana why Vri was staring into her eyes!

"Where I live, the color of my eyes is pretty normal. Nobody has yellow eyes," she said.

They both laughed at that.

"How do you know if someone likes you? I can't imagine loving someone without touching them," Ana asked Vri.

"Um, I don't have my own experience, but my mom and dad told me you just know," answered Vri. "You talk, you spend a lot of time together. And then all of a sudden, your eyes sparkle at the same time and that's it: love. If they don't sparkle, it's not love. Better find someone else. Or others," she laughed. "Sometimes, rarely, there can be more than two people in a marriage."

There was a short pause while they both thought about each other's strange lives.

"Did you kiss with your eyes open or closed?" Vri was the first to break the silence.

What kind of question was that? It was private!

"Closed," Ana answered Vri anyway.

"Maybe if you had opened your eyes, you would have seen that his eyes did not sparkle. You would have known that he was not for you. Maybe next time, you should try kissing with your eyes open," Vri told her.

"Maybe," Ana agreed.

It wasn't bad advice.

CHAPTER 12

"How does the night look?" Vri asked. "There is no night here on Ketan. The sky just darkens a little, and that's all. Is the night really as black as they say?"

"The night sky is black, but not completely black, because the moon shines in it and it is filled with many stars," Ana said. "It's more of a very dark blue. It's completely black only if the night is cloudy, so you can't see the stars and the moon. During the full moon, the night is very bright."

"I would like to see it." Vri sighed longingly. "That is my great wish, to see the night on Earth. When I get permission to travel, it will be the first place I visit!"

"What kind of permission?" Ana asked.

"I must not travel anywhere before my parents agree. And they say that it is still too early, that I am not ready. Maybe they will let me go in a year or two," explained Vri.

If they meant Ketan years, that could mean a whole decade of waiting!

"Can't you just leave?" Ana asked.

"What do you mean? Leave without their permission?" Vri laughed. Such a thought was unbelievable to her.

"I came to Ketan without my mother knowing. She thinks I'm at a friend's house or at the beach or something like that. It's summer, so no one is home all the time," Ana said.

Vri stared at her in complete amazement.

"What? How? But that's... You don't do that!" she said.

"I told you," Ana said. "I want to paint my sea. I need that pigment. It's the most important thing in my life. I planned to come to Ketan, buy the pigment, and immediately head back to Earth. For that I need two days by rocket, measured in Earth time."

This time, the silence lasted longer.

"I have a new plan for you," Vri said, in a different voice. Her eyes turned bright yellow. "You will buy the pigment and return to Earth without it. After you land on Earth, I will open the pigment here, on Ketan. Then I will come to Earth by teleporter with the pigment. That way, you will have almost a whole day to paint the sea."

"Oh, that's fantastic!" Ana said. She wanted to jump with joy.

Was this really happening? Was she dreaming?

"Do you really think so? Would you do that for me?" she asked. "And what about your parents' permission?"

"Don't worry. Leave everything to me. You want to paint your sea, and I want to see the night," Vri said. She seemed confident.

CHAPTER 13

There were no more unpleasant surprises.

Together, they went back to the pigment store, where Ana bought the special blue-green pigment. She told Vri's father that someone else would be coming later to get it and that she wanted the pigment opened then. Vri's father accepted her story without any doubts.

She nodded her goodbye to Vri as if they hardly knew each other and rushed to the train station. Now, she was the one who moved confidently among the crowd. On the train, she got into a pod that fit her height right away. In the rocket, she kindly accepted an extra pillow and a plush friend from the robot flight attendant.

She knew that only half an hour after her landing on Earth, Vri would come through the teleporter in the gray building next to the rocket. And she would have Ana's pigment.

Life was beautiful, after all.

Vri did not let her down. She showed up exactly as agreed and with the pigment in her bag. They would look at the night sky together, and Ana would start painting at dawn the next morning.

Vri was completely fascinated by Earth.

"Colors, colors," she kept saying.

Vri came dressed in warmer clothes because the other Ketans were saying that it was cold on Earth, even in summer.

The sun was just about to set when they went together to the Bay of Waves. They were not alone. Several people were still sunbathing on the beach. Everyone stopped what they were doing and stared at Vri, who was overjoyed by the bay. Her eyes shone with an alien color and intensity.

"What? Have you never seen someone from Ketan before?" Ana shouted at the sunbathers. Vri was too caring to respond in a way that wasn't nice.

"Let's sit down and wait for the sun to set," Ana suggested to her. "Are you cold? Are you hungry?"

Vri shook her head. She looked directly at the sun. None of the humans could do that.

"Do all Earthlings look like this?" Vri asked.

Ana looked at the people on the beach. "No, these are locals, like me. We all look alike," she said. "Our skin is darker in the summer because of the sun. But in the winter, when it's cold and nobody is sunbathing, our skin is very light. We say 'white,' but it's actually a light-beige shade."

"And the hair and the eyes?" Vri asked.

"Our hair is mostly dark brown, but there are also lighter colors. Our eyes are mostly brown, but there are also some blue and green colors," Ana said. "This is not true for all people on Earth, but only for us who live here. When I say 'here,' I mean Europe."

She started to feel like a teacher because of so much explaining.

CHAPTER 14

"What is Europe?" Vri asked.

"Oh, well, that's part of the big land that is surrounded by the big sea," Ana said.

Vri deserved better than that. Ana had to make an effort.

"You know that the Earth is a blue-green globe?" Ana asked. She was trying to be a good teacher.

Vri obediently nodded her head.

Of course she knew. Vri was smarter than Ana.

"Those green parts of the globe, one of those parts is called Europe," Ana explained.

"And all the people living in Europe look like you?" Vri asked.

"No, no. In different parts of Europe, people look very different," Ana said. "I live at the very top of a small peninsula. It's surrounded by a small sea called the Adriatic Sea. People here mostly look like me."

"Why?" Vri asked. "Are other people forbidden to live here?"

"No, they can come and many do, but only during the summer while the sea is still warm," Ana said.

"Is the sea warm now?" Vri asked longingly.

"Yes, in summer the sea temperature reaches as high as 27 degrees Celsius," Ana said.

Vri stared at the sky for a while and then said, "That's not very warm."

"It's warm for humans," Ana explained.

"Tell me more about humans. About your people from the small peninsula," Vri said.

"Well, there is nothing to say," Ana said. "I don't really know much about my people. I don't even feel them as 'mine.'"

There was a clear look of shock on Vri's face.

"I'm not very friendly. It's different from Ketan, I guess," Ana said.

She tried to remember history lessons at school.

"In the past, the Adriatic Sea was important to various conquerors. My small nation would always

52

submit to the stronger one," she said. "Our kitchen is a true reflection of our past. I guess the best of each conqueror was copied and kept."

She finally found something she could brag about.

Really, what can you say positively about a place you want to leave as soon as possible?

CHAPTER 15

"We have no food. We live from the sun. Our skin absorbs heat and converts it into energy," Vri said.

"Food is very important here," Ana said. "If you want to have a successful meeting, the best way is to start it by talking about food. For example, what you ate for lunch or what you ate with your family. Then the other person talks about their lunches and everything ends up with exchanging recipes. Once that part is over, you can start talking about business. Whatever it is, it will be successful after that introduction."

"That's really funny," Vri laughed.

"Yes. Imagine a meeting with a lot of people!

How many recipes will there be?" Ana joined in laughing. "Of course, those meetings end with a lunch. You only get to have one meeting a day."

They burst out laughing.

It was getting darker. Vri wrapped herself in a jacket. She was obviously cold. Everyone left the beach and left them alone.

"What is that in the sky?" Vri asked, pointing. "Moon?"

"Yes. Just a few more minutes and night will fall completely. I have a sweatshirt in my backpack. Want it?" Ana offered.

Vri took the sweatshirt without saying a word and even put the hood over her head.

They sat in silence next to the sea and watched the sky. The sea changed color. It changed from blue-green to dark blue.

"Beautiful," whispered Vri, as if she was afraid that she would drive away the night with her loud voice.

Ana didn't say anything. She wanted her friend to experience the most beautiful night on Earth.

"There it is. A star!" said Vri excitedly "And there! One more! And there! Beautiful, beautiful."

Ana enjoyed Vri's happiness. The evening was romantic: the sunset, the gentle waves of the sea that almost reached their feet, the sky full of stars. To someone seeing it for the first time, it must have looked magical.

CHAPTER 16

Suddenly, Vri turned to Ana and stared at her.

"Your eyes!" Vri said excitedly "Your eyes are like the starry sky!" Vri came close to Ana's face and stared into her eyes.

"Beautiful," she said.

The sweatshirt didn't help her. She was shivering. Ana reached out to hug Vri around the shoulders and warm her.

"No! Don't!" Vri stopped her at the last moment. "I will hurt you!"

"What do you mean? I just want to hug you and warm you," Ana said.

She was surprised. Was Vri afraid of her?

"My skin is very rough. It has scales on it that are sharp," Vri said.

"That's why we Ketans don't touch each other, so we don't scratch each other. And if two Ketans can scratch themselves, imagine what can happen to the delicate skin of humans?"

"You are covered with clothes," Ana said.

"No, I don't want to risk it." Vri was determined. "Here. You can touch me here, but carefully." She held her hand toward Ana with the palm facing up.

Ana cautiously placed her palm on Vri's palm. It was like touching fine sandpaper.

"Okay?" she checked with Vri. She wrapped her fingers around Vri's palm.

There was no sound from Vri because everything was fine. Ana was holding Vri's hand, who was smiling and looking into her eyes.

"Is it like this all over the body? Your skin?" Ana also started whispering, like Vri.

Vri nodded.

Ana felt like she was in the middle of some kind of spell, and all it would take was a small thing to make it disappear.

CHAPTER 17

Ana held Vri's hand, looking into her bright yellow eyes. She saw in them the fascination with her ordinary black eyes. Maybe they weren't so ordinary?

"And here? May I?" she asked.

Vri allowed her to lightly touch her lips with the tips of her fingers. Vri's lips were softer than her palm.

Not even knowing exactly what she was doing, Ana brought her head closer to Vri. Vri was completely calm. She had even stopped shaking from the cold.

Ana slowly placed her lips on Vri's, held them

briefly, and then pulled away from her.

They looked at each other without saying a word.

"That was strange," Ana said first.

"Yes," Vri agreed. "And you closed your eyes again." They both burst out laughing.

"This is the most beautiful day in my life. Ever. I just know." Vri sighed and looked back at the sky. "I want to swim in the sea."

"I'm not sure that's smart," Ana said. She worried about Vri, who was trembling more and more. "The sea is now below 27 degrees Celsius and there is no sun."

Vri glared at her, her yellow eyes twinkling.

"I will only get my feet wet, nothing will happen to me. I'm already cold. Besides, who knows when I will come back to Earth!" she said.

"All right, you know best," Ana said, accepting her friend's decision.

Vri took off her sandals and stepped into the sea. Gentle sea waves lapped at her feet, creating gentle foam. She just stood still and watched the sky.

Then she jumped and ran to the shore. She was shaking so much from the cold that she couldn't get her shoes on.

"Freezing! Freezing!" she cried. She was twitching. "Freet igmirit po! Freet igmirit po!"

"I do not understand! I do not understand! Vri!" Ana shouted. She was beginning to panic. "Speak in my language!"

She took the sandals from Vri and helped her put them on.

"I have to warm up! I need the sun! Sun!" Vri said.

"There will be no sun for at least another five hours. The night has just begun. We can go to my house. You will take a hot shower, I will cover you with all the blankets I have, and you will be warm," Ana said, soothing her.

"Sun! I can't get warm any other way!" Vri said. "I need the sun or I'll die!"

Vri was not exaggerating. Ana saw for herself that the situation was very serious. The color of Vri's skin lightened and her eyes became paler.

CHAPTER 18

"Take me to the solar collector!" demanded Vri.

"We don't have that. That technology is only found in big cities," Ana said.

"I need the sun!" Vri cried out.

What could Ana do? How could she help Vri? She didn't know anyone.

"I'll take you to the teleporter. You will feel your sun in the blink of an eye," she promised Vri.

She ordered a fast taxi and helped Vri to get up. She took off her T-shirt and put it on Vri. The taxi landed on the beach.

Ana somehow got Vri inside the taxi. Vri was barely moving. It was like a kind of numbness began to take over Vri.

"Good evening. Your desired destination is the teleporter," spoke a voice from the speaker. "Is everything okay with the passengers?" There were no drivers, only cameras and sensors that followed passengers' every move.

"We are in a big hurry to get to the teleporter. Please hurry," Ana said, trying to sound calm. If the sensor noticed that something was wrong, it would automatically connect them to the police cameras. She didn't want problems of that kind.

Vri was muttering something Ana couldn't understand. She hugged Vri and tried to comfort her with gentle words. Vri was in such bad condition that she even didn't have the strength to push Ana away because she was touching her.

Ana didn't care if Vri accidentally hurt her. She was ready to do anything to save Vri.

Wearing only a bra with her skirt and holding Vri around the waist so she could walk, Ana entered the gray teleporter building.

She was dazzled by the intensity of the light. She didn't see anyone anywhere. Everything was completely empty.

CHAPTER 19

Ana headed toward the only door she saw. Soon, a robot came to them.

"Good evening." It looked into her eyes to identify her. "Ana Marija Sassi Rizich. How can I help you?"

"My friend urgently needs a teleporter to Ketan. She has a return ticket. Quickly! It's an emergency!" Ana said.

The robot didn't answer. It just stood still. Maybe it decided to make an update at that very moment.

Ana went around it and went on toward the door. A man came out of the door.

"Excuse me! Sorry!" she called without thinking.

The man looked toward them.

"Please!" Ana begged. "We need your help!"

The man walked toward them.

"What happened?" asked the man. He looked between Ana and Vri.

"My friend is freezing. She is from Ketan, she needs the sun," Ana explained. "She needs to go to the teleporter. She has a ticket. Please help us. She will die if she doesn't reach Ketan immediately."

"Good evening. Sorry to interrupt the conversation. I have information for a passenger," the robot said. "The teleporter can leave in five minutes if you still want to travel to Ketan. I just got teleport confirmation."

"Ketan." Vri spoke meaningfully for the first time since they got into the taxi.

Poor thing, she was almost completely pale, and her eyes were a washed-out yellow.

"Please, help me place her in the teleporter. She can't walk," Ana said.

"The passenger can't walk? Passenger with mobility issues?" asked the robot.

"Yes. Yes," Ana said.

The robot transformed into a wheelchair.

"Place the passenger with mobility issues in the seat, please," it said.

Ana carefully placed Vri in the chair and then held her all the way to the only door in the room.

"Entry is allowed only to persons with accreditation and passengers," the robot said.

"But she can't get up! Who will make sure everything is in order? I have to go with her!" Ana cried.

"Please put the accreditation on the screen," the robot insisted. "I don't have accreditation!" Ana said.

"I do," said the man. He placed his wrist on the robot's screen. "You may come in," the robot answered. It started to drive through the door.

"I'll make sure everything is fine," the man promised.

"Wait!" Ana shouted and ran after them.

She couldn't even say goodbye to Vri!

"Vri, forgive me. I would never have let you watch the night if I had known you would be so cold," she called.

Vri just blinked her eyes. She was barely conscious. Maybe she didn't even hear Ana.

The door closed.

CHAPTER 20

Ana was left all alone. She had never felt such loneliness before. One moment, she had a best friend. They were laughing and joking. The next, she was alone.

Exhausted, she sat down on the nearest bench. All kinds of thoughts swarmed in her head. She was worried about Vri.

Would Vri be okay? What if she didn't make it to Ketan on time? What if Vri died?

It was all Ana's fault! If she hadn't desperately wanted to buy the pigment, Vri would now be on Ketan, warmed and happy.

But then they would never have met. And Vri would not have seen the starry sky.

How would Ana know if everything went well? Interplanetary calls were made with a high-tech telephone. She didn't have it. Also, what phone number should she dial? The phone number of the Vri's dad's store? She hoped that Vri's parents would not find out anything about their daughter's adventures.

The door opened and the man who helped them came out.

"Is everything all right?" Ana asked. She ran toward him.

"Yes, yes. I arranged for a special solar collector to be ready for her. On Ketan, they have them on every teleporter, just for situations like this," he explained to her.

"Then do you think everything will be all right?" she asked him hopefully.

"Let's wait a few more minutes," he answered, pointing to the bench where she was sitting.

"Here, this way you will attract less attention," he said. He took off his jacket and handed it to her.

"Thank you," Ana said. She had completely forgotten that she was wearing only a bra.

"Your friend took quite a risk by coming here," the man said.

"Risk? Why? I was on Ketan," Ana said.

"We humans can stay on Ketan with an air

mask and in the shade, but Ketans cannot stay on Earth," he explained. "Our sun is too weak for them. Their skin cools quickly, and they cannot survive on Earth without daily use of solar collectors."

"I didn't know that," Ana said. "She didn't tell me anything."

"I don't think she knew, either. Very few Ketans travel outside their planet precisely because of these temperature limitations. I'm surprised her parents let her do that," he said.

Ana said, "Vri is special."

CHAPTER 21

A slight vibration was heard. The man rubbed his temple and stared at the floor. Interplanetary telephone. He "talked" with his thoughts.

She watched his facial expressions carefully. He was frowning.

"What happened?" Ana asked. She was on the verge of crying.

"Everything went fine. Your friend arrived on Ketan and is now in the solar collector, recovering. She will be okay," he said.

"Then what's wrong?" Ana asked.

"Her parents," he said. "She traveled without their permission. It's serious on Ketan."

"Serious in what way?" Ana asked. "What will happen to her?"

"I do not know," the man said. "Parents decide that. Probably a ban on going out, a ban on travel or socializing. Ketans are very social and find it very difficult to be alone."

She didn't know how to comment on that. She was happy that Vri would be fine. Somehow it seemed to her that the punishment for Vri would not be too severe.

She was pretty sure that Vri knew about all the dangers from the very beginning, when they were sitting on the bench in the park on Ketan. She knew the risk of travel and the risk of punishment. Vri decided to ignore all that in order to see the starry sky.

"Thank you. For everything. I don't know how it would have ended without your help," she told him.

"Well, if I hadn't helped you, you would have found someone else. You seemed very determined. I doubt that anyone would want to argue with such a girl." He was smiling at her.

"Thank you one more time," Ana said. "I don't know how to repay you for all you have done."

"I'm glad I helped," the man said. "My life is planned down to the last detail and without any surprises. In fact, I am grateful to you for this experience. Just stay safe."

Ana returned to the beach again. She didn't feel like sleeping, and she wanted to start painting the sea right at dawn. Vri brought an open pigment, and it would last exactly for that day.

CHAPTER 22

Ana set up everything for the painting and waited. She had imagined that when she opened the pigment and set the canvas on the easel, she would feel inspiration and happiness. No such luck. She didn't feel special at all.

The sky was changing colors from black to deep blue. From pink and orange to a blue sky with a yellow sun.

Vri would really enjoy dawn on Earth.
The sea took on a blue-green color. It was beautiful, but something was missing. She didn't see it as special as before. It had lost its previous charm. Ana spread the pigment on the palette and began to paint with confident brush strokes.

It was finished quickly. She had painted the same landscape too many times to have any trouble. She didn't even use all the pigment. There was too much in the package.

At the end, she sprayed the entire painting with a protective spray. That way, all the colors dried immediately and had stable shades.

She was looking at the finished painting. It was a beautiful landscape with a perfect sea, but she didn't like it.

She set up a new canvas and began to paint a completely new scene. With a lot of love and respect, she painted from memory the starry sky, the moon, the sea, and a small beach. She used all the black and dark-blue pigment she had with her.

She also smudged the canvas with her fingers and spread the paint because she ran out of black toward the end of the painting. And then, she gently added a couple of glitters in the corner of the painting.

An ethereal being. Vri.

When she moved away from the painting and looked at the finished work, she realized that she did not want to be separated from that painting.

The painting was perfect.

CHAPTER 23

Ana stood in line and patiently waited for her turn to board the plane. A dozen people to go before her turn.

It was still hot, and all the passengers were dressed in light summer clothes. Everyone had their wrist monitors turned on. All you had to do was show the monitor to the ticket reader, but for some reason the reader was slow.

She wasn't upset about it. She waited patiently for her turn.

Behind her was a young man who nervously looked over her head and watched what other people were doing in front of them. She guessed that he was her age.

"Traveling for the first time?" she asked him.

"Maybe," he answered with a grin.

She smiled.

"Just do everything I do," she told him when it was her turn.

She placed her wrist on the reader. After a few seconds, the text appeared on the reader:

Ana Marija Sassi Rizich
planet Earth, Europe, 18 years
9 C RIGHT
Destination: Paris

She entered the plane and looked for her seat. She did not stop smiling.

The Paris Academy of Fine Arts, whose competition she had won with the beach-at-night landscape, cooperated with all major pigment stores in the galaxy. This included the pigment store in *Koo' choorb* on Ketan. Vri's dad's store.

She couldn't wait to order the blue-green pigment, noting that it was for painting the Adriatic Sea.

About the Author

Natasa Glisic First is a contributing author to the Storyshares library

About the Publisher